My Little Pony

The Big Book of Equestria

ORCHARD

ORCHARD BOOKS
338 Euston Road
London NW1 3BH
Orchard Books Australia
Level 17/207 Kent Street, Sydney, NSW 2000

First published in 2012 in Italy by Fivestore
This edition published by Orchard Books in 2013

ISBN 978 1 40833 040 1

A CIP catalogue record for this book is available from the British Library.

1 3 5 7 9 10 8 6 4 2

Printed in China

Orchard Books is a division of Hachette Children's Books,
an Hachette UK company.

www.hachette.co.uk

INTRODUCTION

Once upon a time, two unicorn sisters ruled the magical pony land of Equestria. Princess Celestia raised the sun at dawn, and Princess Luna brought out the moon to begin the night.

But Princess Luna grew unhappy. The ponies were never awake to enjoy her beautiful night. Her anger turned her into a wicked witch called Night Mare Moon, and she vowed to make the night last for ever.

Princess Celestia used powerful magic to banish her wicked sister to the moon. But Night Mare Moon was determined to return to Equestria and plunge the land into eternal darkness . . .

Friendship is Magic

It was a big day in Equestria. All the ponies in the kingdom were enjoying a grand party in honour of Princess Celestia, the Queen of Equestria.

Suddenly a shadow fell across the party. Night Mare Moon had escaped her banishment and returned to Equestria! She used her evil magic to throw the kingdom into darkness, then disappeared in a puff of violet smoke – taking the queen with her!

"I must save the queen!" cried Twilight Sparkle.

"We'll help you!" said her friends Rarity, Applejack, Fluttershy, Pinkie Pie and Rainbow Dash.

"There's only one way to defeat Night Mare Moon," said Twilight Sparkle. "We need the six Elements of Harmony. Five of the elements are known: honesty, kindness, laughter, generosity and loyalty. The sixth element is a mystery. The last known location of the Elements was in the ancient castle of the royal unicorn sisters – in Everfree Forest."

Everfree Forest was a creepy place. But if the pony friends were going to save Princess Celestia, they had to be brave.

As the six ponies trotted into the dark forest, Night Mare Moon opened a huge hole in the ground to swallow them up. Twilight Sparkle lost her footing and slipped into the hole.

"What do I do?" she cried in panic.

"Trust me," said Applejack. "You'll be safe, I promise."

Twilight Sparkle trusted Applejack. She held on tight . . . and Applejack pulled her to safety.

Next, Night Mare Moon sent
a giant lion to stop the ponies.
It snarled and roared, and the
ponies all panicked . . . all except
Fluttershy.

"Shh," she said in a soft voice.
"It's okay." She could see that the
lion had a thorn in his paw. Bravely
she stepped forward and pulled out
the thorn. The lion started to purr!

"Sometimes we all just need
to be shown a little kindness,"
said Fluttershy.

Suddenly all the trees in the
forest turned into scary monsters.

"Run!" cried Twilight Sparkle.

But Pinkie Pie refused to run. Instead, she began to laugh and sing.
Her song was so much fun that the other ponies started to laugh
too, and their laughter was stronger than Night Mare Moon's
magic. Soon the trees returned to normal.

Beside a river, the ponies found a sea serpent who was sobbing unhappily.

"A cloud of purple smoke just whisked past and tore off half my moustache!" sniffed the poor serpent. "Now I look awful."

The other ponies thought the serpent was being silly, but Rarity understood. He just wanted to look his best. She took a deep breath . . . and cut a lock from her tail to mend his moustache!

"There. You look wonderful," she said.

"Oh, thank you," said the serpent. "Here, let me help you cross the river."

At last Night Mare Moon's ruined castle was in sight, but the footbridge to the entrance was broken.

"Don't worry, I'll fix it!" said Rainbow Dash. As she zoomed into the air, she heard someone calling her name. Looking up, she saw the captain of the Wonder Bolts, her favourite acrobatic team!

"Leave your friends and come and join my team," said the captain.

Rainbow Dash was amazed. She had always wanted to join the Wonder Bolts! She had no idea that it wasn't the captain of the team at all, but Night Mare Moon in disguise, trying to keep the ponies away from the castle.

"Thank you for the offer," said Rainbow Dash politely, "but I have to say no. I'd never leave my friends."

As soon as the bridge was mended, the ponies entered the ancient ruin. They searched each dusty room until they found five sparkling jewels.

"The Elements of Harmony!" squealed Twilight Sparkle.

"Where's the sixth element?" asked Rainbow Dash.

"The book said, 'When the five elements are present, a spark will cause the sixth element to be revealed'," Twilight Sparkle remembered.

Suddenly Twilight Sparkle and the gemstones vanished. They were transported to another room in the ruin . . . with Night Mare Moon.

The evil unicorn smashed the Elements of Harmony with her hooves.

"Now you will never see your queen or your sun again," she cried. "The night will last for ever!"

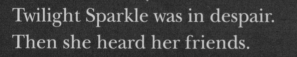

Twilight Sparkle was in despair.
Then she heard her friends.

"Hang on!" they called.
"We're coming!"

Suddenly Twilight Sparkle
understood everything.
"The Elements of Harmony
are right here!" she cried.

"What?" snapped
Night Mare Moon.

"The spirits of my five friends got us through every challenge you threw at us," said Twilight Sparkle. "Applejack's *honesty*, Fluttershy's *kindness*, Pinkie Pie's *laughter*, Rarity's *generosity* and Rainbow Dash's *loyalty*."

"You still don't have the sixth element!" said Night Mare Moon.

Twilight Sparkle laughed. "Those five elements are ignited by the spark of friendship in our hearts," she said. "It creates the sixth element – the element of magic!"

Suddenly a beautiful rainbow surrounded everyone and Princess Celestia appeared. She was free! But something even more magical had happened. The wicked witch was gone! Night Mare Moon had turned back into Princess Luna.

The sisters hugged each other. Then Princess Celestia turned to Twilight Sparkle and her friends. "Thank you," she said. "Thanks to you brave ponies, the sun will shine on Equestria for ever!"

The Sonic Rainboom

"I wish you guys were able to fly to Cloudsdale to see me compete in the Best Young Flyer competition," Rainbow Dash said to her friends.

She was very excited. The competition was her chance to show off her flying skills in front of her favourite acrobatic team, the Wonder Bolts.

When a Pegasus pony flies fast enough, a sonic boom and a rainbow can happen at the same time, creating a Sonic Rainboom. Rainbow Dash was determined to perform a Sonic Rainboom for the competition. There was just one problem – no matter how much she practised, she never could do it!

Rainbow Dash's friends could see that she was nervous, and wanted to help her.

"Can you find a spell that will get us wingless ponies into Cloudsdale?" Rarity begged Twilight Sparkle. "I've put on enough fashion shows to recognise stage fright when I see it."

Twilight Sparkle searched her
books until she found a spell that
would allow herself, Applejack
and Pinkie Pie to walk on
clouds. Then she made Rarity a
magnificent pair of wings spun
from gossamer and dew.

Rainbow Dash couldn't believe her eyes when her friends arrived in Cloudsdale.

"This is so cool!" she said. "I was starting to get just the teeniest tiniest bit nervous, but I feel a lot better now that you guys are here."

Rainbow Dash took her friends to visit Cloudsdale's famous Weather Factory, where snowflakes and rainbows are made. The friends kept being stopped by ponies who wanted to admire Rarity's wings.

"*You* should enter the competition," said one of the ponies. "I could watch you fly all day long!"

Rarity was very flattered. "They *are* beautiful wings," she said. "Perhaps I *should* compete."

Rainbow Dash started to feel worried. "I can't do the Sonic Rainboom," she said, "and just look at these boring old wings. I'll never win the competition."

But there was no time to back out now. The competition was about to start!

At the Cloudsdale Stadium, the announcer introduced the celebrity judges for the Best Young Flyer competition – the Wonder Bolts. The crowd went wild as the famous team arrived.

The other contestants performed their routines, and at last it was Rainbow Dash's turn. But the stage manager had bad news.

"There's only time for one more performance," she said to Rarity and Rainbow Dash. "If you both want to compete, you'll just have to go out there together."

Rarity put on a wonderful performance, but everything Rainbow Dash tried seemed to go wrong.

Then Rarity made an announcement. "I will fly right up to the sun!" she declared, and she began to flutter upwards on her beautiful wings.

"Looks like this is my last chance to turn things around," Rainbow Dash said to herself. "It's time for the Sonic Rainboom. Wings, don't fail me now!"

Suddenly Rarity screamed. Her thin wings had melted in the sunlight, and she was falling! The Wonder Bolts flew to help her, but Rarity's flailing hooves knocked them all out. Now the Wonder Bolts were falling too!

"Hold on, Rarity!" shouted Rainbow Dash. "I'm coming!"

Rainbow Dash flew faster than ever
before. Suddenly, as she shot through the
air – BOOM! – she did a perfect Sonic
Rainboom! The crowd gasped as she caught
Rarity and the Wonder Bolts just before they
hit the ground.

"Thank you, Rainbow Dash!" gasped Rarity.
"You saved my life!"

The audience went wild, cheering and shouting
for Rainbow Dash.

Rarity hugged Rainbow Dash. "I want to apologise for getting so carried away with my beautiful wings," she said.

"It's okay, everything turned out all right," said Rainbow Dash with a smile.

Princess Celestia stepped onto the stage to announce the winner.

"For her incredible bravery, and her spectacular Sonic Rainboom, I'm presenting the grand prize for Best Young Flyer to Rainbow Dash!" she said.

All her friends whooped and cheered.

"This is the BEST DAY EVER!" said Rainbow Dash.

BOAST BUSTERS

One morning, as Twilight Sparkle and Spike were walking through Ponyville, their friends Snails and Snips dashed up to them.

"There's a new unicorn in town!" cried Snails.

"They say she's got more magical powers than any other unicorn ever!" added Snips.

Spike thought Twilight Sparkle was the most magical unicorn in Equestria. She knew all kinds of amazing spells – once she'd even given Spike a wonderful magic moustache! "I don't like the sound of this new unicorn," he thought.

The new unicorn was called Trixie, and she had set up her magic show in the town square. Snips and Snails led the way.

"Come one, come all!" Trixie shouted. "Come and witness the amazing magic of the great and powerful Trixie!"

Twilight Sparkle's friends didn't think much of Trixie.

"What a show-off!" said Rarity.

"Yeah," said Spike. "We all know that Twilight Sparkle is the most powerful magician in Equestria."

"Shh!" said Twilight Sparkle, pulling Spike to one side. "I don't want anyone thinking *I'm* a show-off like Trixie."

Trixie overheard what the ponies were saying about her and felt cross.

"Who dares to challenge the magical ability of the great and powerful Trixie?" she demanded. "Don't they know that they are in the presence of the most magical unicorn in all of Equestria?"

"What makes you think you're so great anyway?" asked Rainbow Dash.

Trixie glared at Rainbow Dash. "I am the best wizard in the world. No one but ME could defeat the giant bear Ursa Major with the flick of a hoof!"

Trixie began to use her magic to make fun of the ponies. Applejack was tied up, Rainbow Dash got in a spin and Rarity's hair turned green. But Twilight Sparkle crept away. She didn't want to get into a quarrel with Trixie, and she certainly didn't want her friends to think she was a show-off.

Spike found Twilight Sparkle in the library. "Your magic is much stronger than that show-off Trixie," he said. "You should teach her a lesson!"

"No," replied Twilight Sparkle. "Didn't you see what everyone thought of Trixie's boasting? If I go out there and show off my magic, my friends will think I'm bragging too."

Meanwhile, Snips and Snails had been thinking about what Trixie had said. They wanted to see her powerful magic for themselves! So, as night fell across Ponyville, they crept into Everfree Forest to find a giant bear for Trixie to defeat. They searched the dark forest until they found an Ursa Major sleeping in a cave. It woke up and let out a loud roar. Then it chased Snips and Snails all the way back to Ponyville!

The Ursa Major thundered into Ponyville, crushing houses and flattening everything in its path.

"Help us, Great and Powerful Trixie!" cried Snails. "You must defeat the Ursa!"

Trixie looked very worried. "Er, okay," she said. "Piece of cake. Stand back."

Trixie conjured up a lightning bolt to strike the Ursa Major. But he hardly noticed it!

"Come on, Trixie!" said Snips.

"Stop messing around and defeat it!" added Snails.

Trixie had to tell the truth. "No one can defeat an Ursa Major!" she said. "I just made the whole story up to make me look better!"

"I'll take care of this," said Twilight Sparkle.

She moved through the crowd, casting spells. First she soothed the Ursa Major with an enchanted lullaby. Then she gave him a bottle of warm milk. As he drifted off to sleep, she used her magic to send him back to his cave in the forest. All the ponies gasped and cheered.

"Please don't think badly of me," said Twilight Sparkle as her friends gathered round. "I know how much Trixie's showing off with *her* magic tricks annoyed you all."

"Your magic is a part of who you are," said Applejack. "We're proud to have such a powerful, talented unicorn as our friend."

"So it IS possible to defeat an Ursa Major all by yourself!" said Spike.

"That wasn't an Ursa Major," said Twilight Sparkle. "It was just a baby. An Ursa *Minor.*"

Trixie looked very embarrassed. She quickly packed up her magic show and left Ponyville before anyone could make her face up to her mistakes!

Snips and Snails agreed to clean up the mess in Ponyville as a punishment for all the trouble they'd caused. And Twilight Sparkle shared a hug with her friends. "I have learnt a very valuable lesson," she said. "It's okay to be proud of your talents. And there are times when it's good to show them off, *especially* when you are standing up for your friends!"

SWARM OF THE CENTURY

Everyone in Ponyville was very excited. Princess Celestia was coming for a visit the following day, and the ponies were throwing a magnificent party in her honour.

Fluttershy and her animal friends were gathering flowers for a special bouquet.

"Remember, these flowers are for Princess Celestia," she told them. "Only the prettiest ones will do."

Suddenly Fluttershy saw a funny little insect. "Hello, little guy," she said. "I've never seen anything like you before. Are you hungry?"

Spotting a tub of apples, the insect dived in . . . and ate them all up! Then it snuggled sleepily into Fluttershy's mane

"I guess you *were* hungry," said Fluttershy with a giggle. "You're the cutest thing ever! I can't wait to show you to my friends."

Twilight Sparkle was at the Sugarcube Sweet Shoppe, making sure that everything was ready for the party. She found Pinkie Pie tasting all the cakes that had been made for the princess!

"It's the only way to make sure they're good enough for royalty!" said Pinkie Pie, gulping down another cupcake.

Just then, Fluttershy raced into the shop.
"Twilight! Pinkie!" she cried. "Look what I found!"

But instead of one insect coming out of
her mane, three appeared! Twilight Sparkle
thought they were adorable, but Pinkie Pie
looked worried.

"UGH!" she said. "A Parasprite! Now I've
got to find a trombone." She hurried off,
leaving her friends feeling very confused.

In Rarity's shop, Carousel Couture, Rainbow Dash was being fitted for a brand new outfit. Fluttershy and Twilight Sparkle arrived with *six* insects.

"Ooh, can I have one?" asked Rainbow Dash.

"Me too!" said Rarity. "They're so sweet!"

That night, all the ponies went to bed early. The princess was arriving the next day and everyone wanted to look their best. But when the residents of Ponyville woke up the next morning, they got a terrible shock. The little insects were everywhere, and they were eating every bit of food in the village!

"I know what to do," said Twilight Sparkle. "I'll cast a spell to make the insects stop eating all the food!"

The spell worked – the insects stopped eating the food. But then they started eating everything else instead! They devoured carts, signs, walls and even Rarity's clothes. Ponyville was disappearing!

"Does anyone know where I can find a banjo?" said Pinkie Pie.

But her friends weren't listening. They were much too busy trying to stop the insects eating everything in sight. Applejack tried rounding them up, but the little creatures kept escaping.

Rainbow Dash tried flying in a circle to create a tornado. It captured the insects and started to carry them out of Ponyville. But just as they reached the edge of the village, the tornado broke up and the insects were free again.

Pinkie Pie raced up. "Have you got an accordion?" she asked.

"Will you forget about your silly instruments for one second?" said Rainbow Dash in a cross voice. "We're trying to save Ponyville!"

"So am I!" Pinkie Pie complained. "LISTEN TO ME!"

But no one had time to listen. Princess Celestia was on her way!

Feeling desperate, Twilight Sparkle visited her wise friend Zecora the Zebra in Everfree Forest.

"These little guys are devouring Ponyville!" she said. "And the princess is on her way! Can you help us?"

Zecora always spoke in rhyme: *"Tales of crops and harvests consumed. If these creatures are in Ponyville . . . you're doomed."*

Feeling even worse, Twilight Sparkle raced back towards Ponyville. Suddenly she heard the sound of music. Pinkie Pie was walking through the village, playing all the instruments she had collected.

"We're in the middle of a crisis here!" exclaimed Twilight Sparkle. "This is no time for your nonsense!"

But when the little insects heard the music, they started to follow Pinkie Pie. She led them out of Ponyville, and they all flew away. Ponyville was saved!

Princess Celestia landed beside the ponies. "I'm terribly honoured that you and the good citizens of Ponyville have organised a parade in honour of my visit," she said. "Unfortunately an emergency has come up in Fillydelphia. I'll have to visit another time."

Twilight Sparkle gave a relieved smile. Now they had time to tidy up the village! The princess said goodbye and flew away.

"So you knew what those critters were all along, huh, Pinkie Pie?" asked Applejack.

"Why do you think I was so frantic to get my hooves on all these instruments?" said Pinkie Pie. "I tried to tell you!"

"We're sorry we didn't listen," said Twilight Sparkle. "You're a great friend, even if we don't always understand you."

"Thank you," said Pinkie Pie. "You're all great friends, too – even when *I* don't understand me!"

THE BEST NIGHT EVER

"The Grand Galloping Gala!" squealed Spike the dragon. "Twilight Sparkle, look! Two invitations for *you*!"

The Grand Galloping Gala was the biggest, most exciting celebration in the realm of Equestria. When Twilight Sparkle told her friends the news, they all wanted the spare ticket.

"Whoever has the best reason to go to the gala should get the ticket," said Twilight Sparkle.

"The Wonder Bolts will be there," said Rainbow Dash. "I'd love to meet them!"

"I'd like to sell apples from my farm," said Applejack.

"I might meet a handsome prince," sighed Rarity.

"I could try new cakes and make new friends!" cried Pinkie Pie.

"I could visit the animals in the castle garden!" said Fluttershy.

But Twilight Sparkle could only take one friend with her. How could she decide who to pick?

Twilight Sparkle's friends wouldn't give her a moment's peace. They followed her around. They gave her presents. They argued with each other.

"I never thought being showered with favours would be so *annoying*," said Twilight Sparkle. "I've had enough of this. If we can't all go, I won't go either!"

Twilight Sparkle's friends felt ashamed of themselves.

"Twilight, you don't have to do that!" said Applejack.

But Twilight Sparkle had made up her mind. "It's okay, girls," she said. "I couldn't possibly enjoy myself without my best friends there with me."

She sent the invitations back to Princess Celestia, and explained why she couldn't come.

Princess Celestia's reply was very quick. She sent six invitations – one for each of Twilight Sparkle's best friends!

Now all the ponies could go and make their dreams come true!

The ponies wanted to look their best for the gala. In her shop, Carousel Couture, Rarity worked hard to make glamorous new outfits for each of her friends. She designed, cut and sewed for weeks, making each pony the perfect gown for the gala.

At last the evening of the gala arrived. The ponies arranged their hair and put on their outfits. Then Spike drove them to Canterlot Castle.

"I can't believe we're finally here!" said Twilight Sparkle.

Each pony was ready for her dreams to come true at the gala.

It was a wonderful party. Twilight Sparkle happily greeted Princess Celestia, Rarity met a handsome stallion prince, and Applejack sold the first of her apple goodies. Rainbow Dash was invited to hang out with the Wonder Bolts, Fluttershy heard a meadowlark singing in the garden, and Pinkie Pie tried three new cakes.

But after a while, the party became less exciting. The music was so noisy that Rainbow Dash couldn't make the Wonder Bolts hear what she was saying. Rarity's handsome stallion was proud and vain, and no one wanted to dance with Pinkie Pie. In the castle garden, the animals were too shy to come close to Fluttershy. Even Applejack was unhappy – no one was buying her wonderful goodies.

Twilight Sparkle was trying to talk to Princess Celestia,
but they kept being interrupted by other guests.

"This isn't what I imagined," Twilight Sparkle said to herself.

But the six ponies weren't going to give up on their dreams so easily.
"If it's the last thing we do, we're going to make this the best night
ever!" they all exclaimed.

The ponies tried to make the party more fun. Pinkie Pie started dancing – but she accidentally sent one of Applejack's apple cakes flying through the air. It hit the vain prince, who backed into a statue. Rainbow Dash darted through the air to catch the statue, but she lost her balance and hit a pillar.

Like dominoes, all the pillars in the ballroom collapsed. At that moment, Fluttershy chased a crowd of terrified animals into the room. It was pandemonium!

Princess Celestia looked at Twilight Sparkle. "Run," she whispered.

The ponies found Spike in the Canterlot Doughnut Shop. Their pretty outfits were ruined, but when they told Spike what had happened, they suddenly saw the funny side of it!

"I just hope Princess Celestia isn't upset with us for ruining the gala," said Twilight Sparkle.

At that moment, Princess Celestia walked into the shop and smiled at them. She had been hoping that the ponies would liven things up a bit!

"In the end, it didn't turn out so bad for this group of friends," she said.

"Friends can find the fun in any situation," Twilight Sparkle agreed.

Being together had made it all better. In fact, it *was* the best night ever!

COLOUR, STICK AND PLAY WITH MY LITTLE PONY!

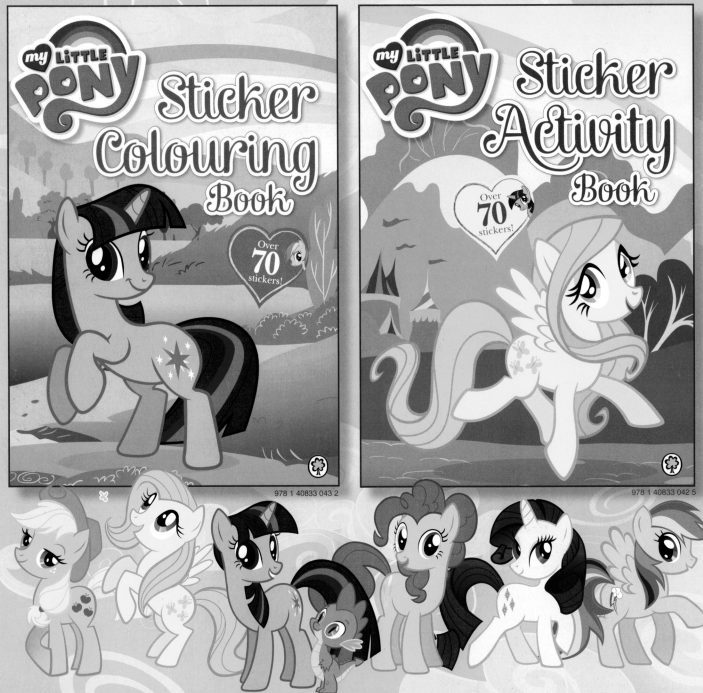

978 1 40833 043 2

978 1 40833 042 5

Orchard books are available from all good bookshops.
They can be ordered via our website: www.orchardbooks.co.uk,
or by telephone: 01235 827 702, or fax: 01235 827 703

ORCHARD